K is for Krakow
The ABCs of Krakow Poland

by Nina R. Bac

Copyright ©2024 by Nina R. Bac

ISBN: 978-1-963177-84-8
Paperback ISBN: 978-1-963177-85-5
Hardback; 978-1-964818-44-3

All rights reserved.

No part of the this book may be reproduced or used in any manner without thw written permission of the copyright owner, except for the use of brief quotations in a book review.

This book is dedicated to the Bac family, who have provided me with constant love and support.

All photos are the sole property of the author. All pictures were taken by the author and enhanced with watercolor using the Waterlogue Pro app.

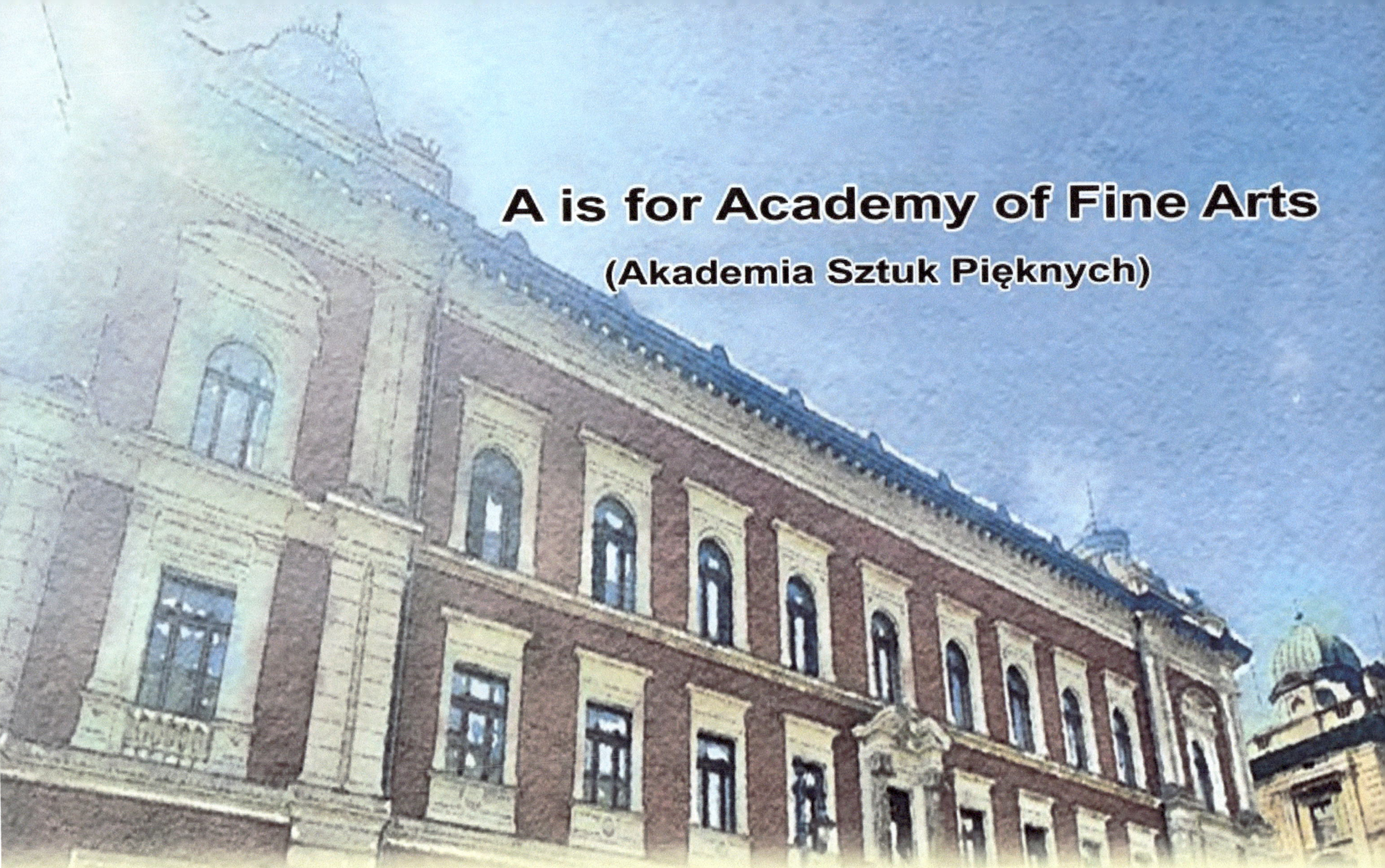

A is for Academy of Fine Arts
(Akademia Sztuk Pięknych)

The Jan Matejko Academy of Fine Arts in Krakow is the oldest Polish fine art academy, established in 1818 as a public institution of higher education.

B is for Barbican
(Barbakan Krakowski)

The Barbican was constructed in the late 15th century as a defense for the main entrance of Kraków.

C is for Cloth Hall
(Sukiennice)

The Cloth Hall, located in the main square, is the world's oldest shopping mall dating back to the Renaissance, and features many small shops in its interior.

D is for Dragon Statue
(Pomnik Smoka Wawelskiego)

Located under the Krakow Wawel Hill, the Dragon's Den is the legendary hideout of the Wawel Dragon, one of Krakow's most famous symbols.

E is for Eagle
(Orzeł)

The white eagle is the national symbol of Poland and is the central element of the Polish coat of arms and crest.

F is for Floriańska Gate
(Brama Floriańska)

The Medieval city walls were built in the 14th century as part of the city's fortifications against attack. Today, an open-air art gallery is exhibited on the side of the Floriańska Gate.

G is for Gargoyles
(Gargulce)

Gargoyles are believed to offer protection to the structures they watch over, such as the Juliusz Słowacki Theatre, a 19th-century theatre and opera house.

H is for Horse-drawn carriage rides
(dorożki konne)

Horse-drawn carriage rides are popular attractions in Krakow and can be found lined up along the market square.

I is for Institute of National Remembrance
(Instytut Pamięci Narodowej)

The Institute's mission is to research and promote Poland's modern history.

J is for Jagiellonian University

The Jagiellonian University, established in 1364 by the Polish King Casimir III the Great, is one of the oldest higher education institutions in Europe and Poland.

K is for Kazimierz

The area formerly known as the Jewish Quarter is now a bustling hub of charming restaurants, local markets, and historical landmarks.

L is for Little Market Square
(Mały Rynek)

One of the most scenic places in Krakow is the Little Market, which used to be a meat market during the Middle Ages and is now located just a block away from the Main Market Square.

M is for Main Market Square
(Rynek Główny)

The largest Medieval town square in Europe is located at the center of the city.

N is for National Museum
(Muzeum Narodowe w Krakowie)

Founded in 1879, the museum is Poland's largest and features a diverse collection of art, ranging from classical archeology to modern works, with a particular emphasis on Polish paintings.

O is for Old Kleparz
(Stary Kleparz)

This market selling locally grown produce has been around for more than 800 years.

P is for Planty Park

Planty Park is a vast urban park that surrounds the Old Town in Kraków.

Q is for Queen Jadwiga's Footprint
(stópka Królowej Jadwigi)

There is a footprint of Queen Jadwiga (AD 1390) on the wall of Church Na Piasku. The footprint is a commemoration of her kind heart. According to legend, the Queen was giving a golden clasp from her slipper to a stonemason when she stepped on a stone, leaving her footprint behind.

R is for River Vistula
(rzeka Wisła)

Krakow is defined by the Vistula River, the longest in Poland, which holds great symbolic significance for the country's culture, history, and national identity.

S is for Saints Peter and Paul Church
(Kościół Świętych Piotra i Pawła)

The Church of Saints Peter and Paul, serving the Catholic parish, was buit on Grodzka Street between 1597 amd 1619.

T is for Theater Bagatela
(Teatr Bagatela)

The theater, which opened in 1919, is located at the intersection of Karmelicka Street and Krupniczej Street and currently hosts musicals, comedies, and other light entertainment shows.

U is for U.S. Consulate

The U.S. Consulate in Krakow provides services for U.S. citizens living or traveling in Krakow, including passport renewal and birth registration.

V is for Victory Monument
(Pomnik Grunwaldzki)

The Grunwald Monument commemorates Poland's victory in the Battle of Grunwald in 1410 against the Teutonic Order.

W is for Wawel Royal Castle
(Zamek Królewski na Wawelu)

The Wawel Royal Castle was a residence for Polish kings for centuries and is now a top art museum in the country.

40 M. CSABA COMMAND A.C. - RUSSIA 1942-43

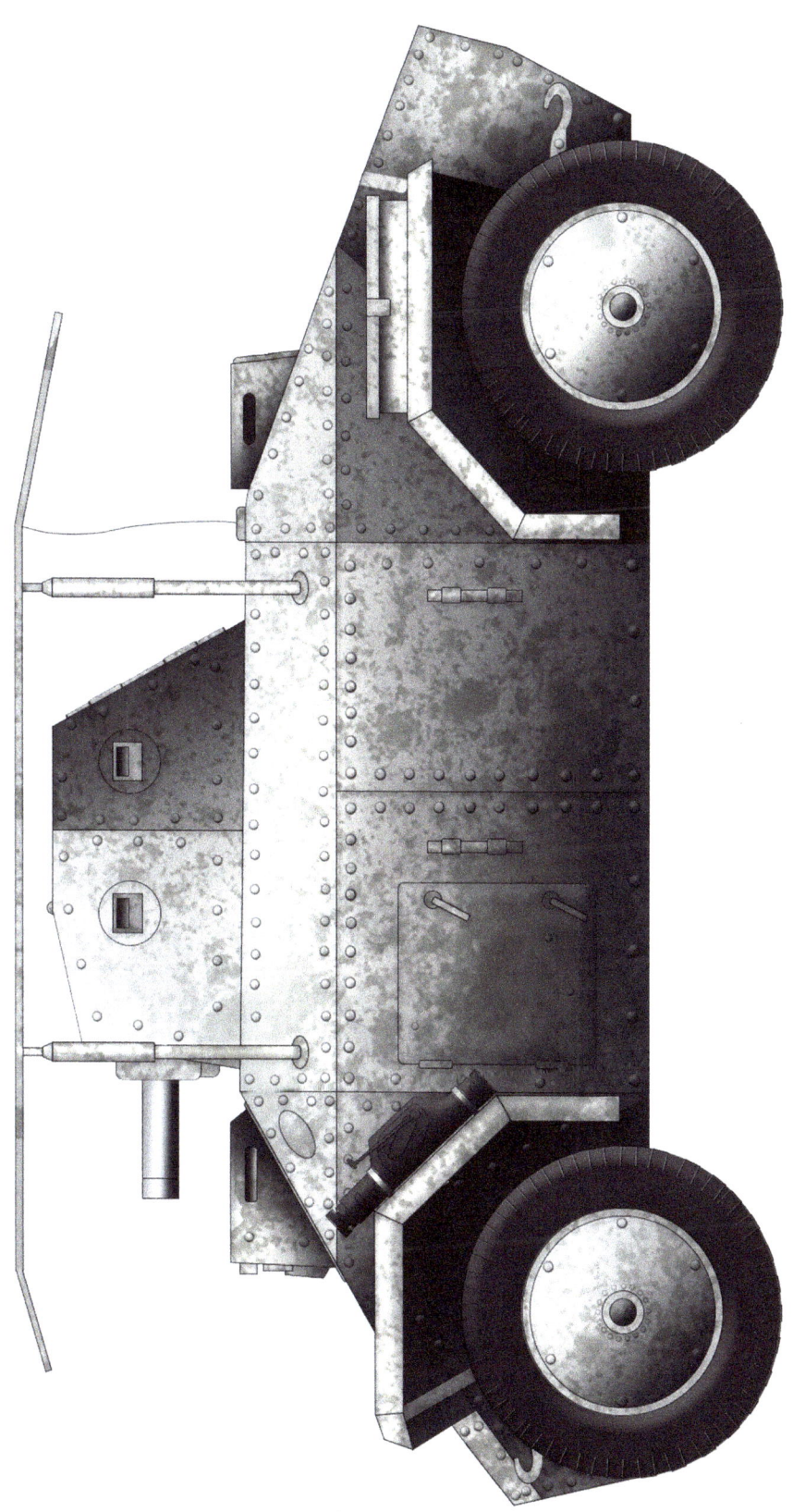

▲ Winter camouflaged 40 M. Csaba command/signal armoured car belonged to the 1st Reconnaissance Battalion fought during the winter battle at the River Don 1942-1943.

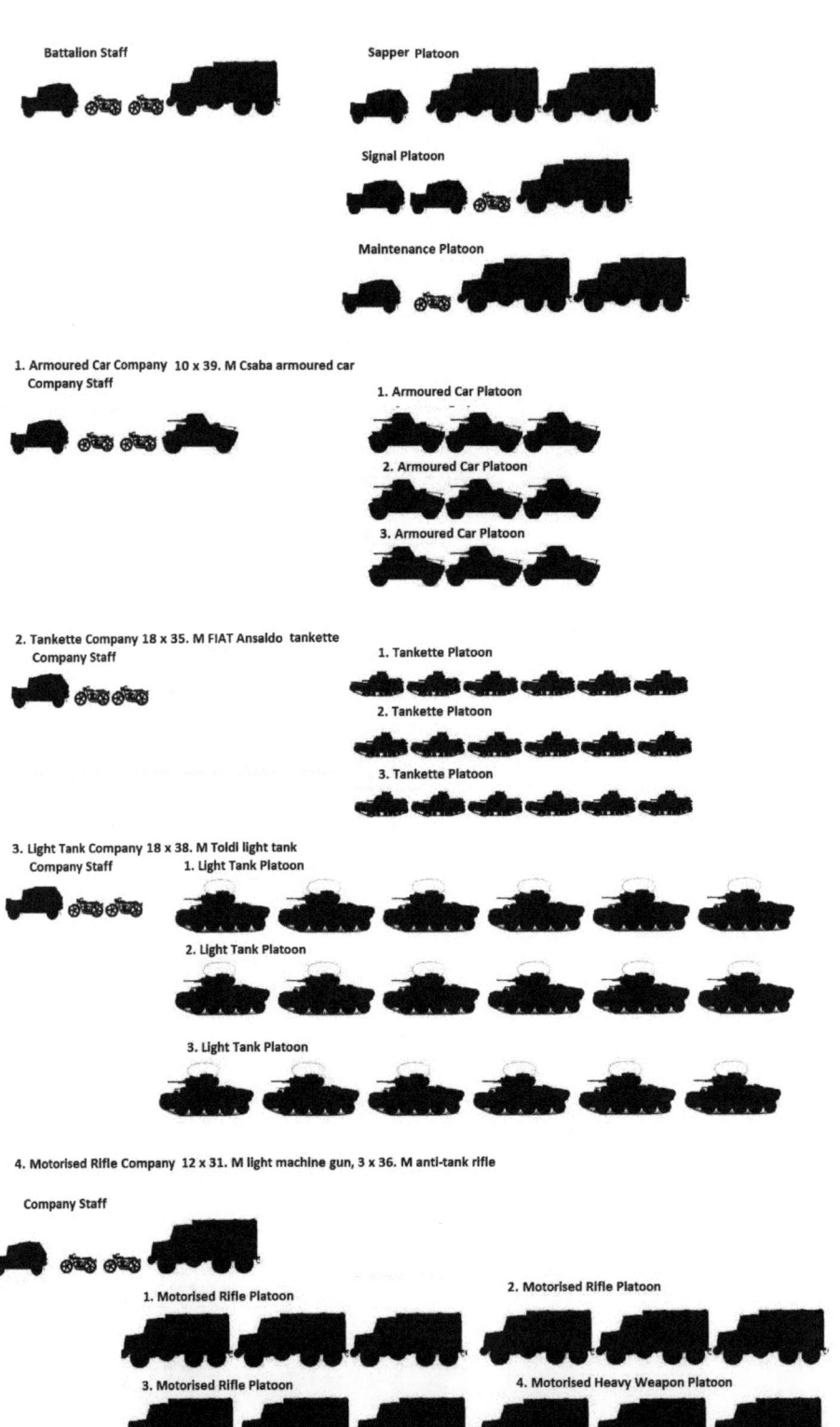

favour of the Hungarian military leadership. Under the guidance of the HTI, the engineers of the Weiss Manfréd Factory utilised the A.C.2 armoured car chassis, Hungarian designed superstructure was constructed, which became the pre-type of the modern Hungarian armoured car. The Hungarian armoured vehicle was given the license plate P-19, which was one of the Weiss Manfred Factory's test vehicles. Its hull differed significantly from the rounded version designed for the British vehicle. The A.C. Alvis superstructure designed for A.C.3 only became known in Csepel in 1938, so it is not known how much it affected the shape of the later 39 M. Csaba armoured car. The later Csaba turret was certainly formed here with small differences, and the arrangement of the weapon installation also became final. The Hungarian Chief of Staff first tried to procure armoured cars through foreign purchases. The Austrian ADKZ, the Swedish Lynx and some German armoured vehicles seemed to be the right type, but - as in the case of tanks - the high purchase price, precarious international situation and the German reluctance to sell complicated the business.

Simultaneously with the foreign procurement, the Weiss Manfréd Factory submitted its production offer based on an armoured car in its possession. It was the prototype of the A.C. armoured car designed by Nicholas Straussler and the engineers of the Weiss Manfred Company.

The Weiss Manfréd's offer included the chassis, engine and running gear, but it also seemed suitable for construction with an armoured superstructure. The uncertainty surrounding foreign purchases, the deteriorating international situation, and the urgency of preparing for war forced the military leadership to accept the domestic production.

In the summer of 1938, the Hungarian Chief of Staff supporting the development of an indigenous armoured vehicle based on the A.C.2 armoured car design. The Weiss Manfréd Factory was commissioned to prepare the prototype. After operational trials with the prototype, in early 1939, the modified A.C.2 was adopted as a 39 M. Csaba armoured car, and by the end of the year, the production of the first series was ordered.

■ TECHNICAL FEATURES

Hull and turret

The hull of the Csaba armoured car was divided into driver, turret and engine compartment. The Csaba's angularly-shaped body with no vertical plates was designed to give extra protection to the crew and engine by deflecting projectiles and shrapnel. The turret likewise was formed with angled armour plates. On the hull of the armoured car, at front and rear, mudguards were fixed which provided space for storage boxes, entrenching tools, jacks. The armoured car had two driver's seats with the same control panels at the front and rear of the car, although the rear driver's seat was very narrow and squeezed to the left due to the engine situated at the rear of the car. The drivers were protected by an armoured cupola (called a helmet) which could be opened and lowered according to the combat situation. The driver's seat was adjustable by the drivers while driving the car. With a closed driving cupola, the drivers orientated through periscopes. The Csaba armoured car had a hexagonal shape centrally-positioned turret that rotated 360°. The side plates of the turret got observation ports. The rear turret plate accommodated a large double door with two observation ports too. The turret also had a roof hatch for the commander. The frontal plate accommodated the weapons of the armoured car. The 34/37 M. machine gun and its sight were built in the right weapon port and the 36 M. anti-tank rifle and its sight in the left one.

Armament

The turret fitted with a 20mm 36 M. anti-tank rifle and an 8mm Gebauer 34/37 M. machine gun. Also, on board was a removable 8mm Solothurn 31 M. light machine gun that could fire through the rear hatch of the turret as an antiaircraft weapon. The vehicle carried 200 rounds for the anti-tank rifle and 3000 rounds for the machine guns. The Hungarian 20mm 36 M. anti-tank rifle was based on the Swiss Solothurn S-18/100 design. Its muzzle velocity was 762m/s. The projectile, the Hungarian AP (armour-piercing) shell, could pierce 20mm armour angled at 60° from 100m, and 16mm of armour angled at 60° from

500m. The weapon had a five rounds magazine and could fire 10-20 rounds per minute. The Hungarian 8mm 34/37 M. Gebauer machine gun had a 25 rounds magazine and fired 8x56mmR ammunition. The 8mm Solothurn 31 M. light machine gun also fired 8x56mmR ammunition. Its magazine held 25 rounds, and the weapon's rate of fire was a moderate 350 rounds per minute. Every crew member had a 9mm 37 M. service pistol for self-defence, two 8mm 31 M. carbines and hand grenades were stored too. Later, 35 M. rifles and 39 and 43 M. sub-machine guns were added to the weaponry.

Crew
It was manned by a crew of four comprising commander, gunner, front driver, and rear driver/radio operator. The Csaba had a tight fighting compartment especially when the crew wearing their leather protective suits. However, according to battlefield records, the Csaba armoured cars regularly evacuated their comrades from the damaged vehicles cramped six to eight men into their armoured cars.

Radio
The 39 M. Csaba armoured car was equipped with an R/4 radio which operated using a frame antenna mounted outside the car body and a telescopic stick antenna built into the rear armour on the left side of the turret. It was operated by the rear driver/radioman.

Armour
The armour of the vehicle, built of riveted and bolted armour plates, with a thickness of 13 mm on the front, 9 mm on the car body, and 7 mm on the cover plate. The vertical plates of the driver's cupola were also made with 13mm armour. The turret had 9mm armour plates too.

Engine
The armoured car was operated with a 90Hp V-8 German Ford engine positioned in the rear of the hull. The 90-horsepower, overdrive, 8-cylinder, in-line engine allowed the vehicle to move forward and backward with its 5-5-speed transmission system. The fuel was stored in a lower 120-litre fuel tank situated under the hull and a spare 15-litre fuel tank situated behind the rear armoured plate.

Suspension
The Csaba had independent suspension, two and four-wheel drive, and four-wheel steering which could be set to front or rear two-wheel steering. These attributes gave the Csaba excellent off-road capabilities but required rather involved maintenance. The vehicle, which rode on four large 22x9,75 (1100 mm) tires, with servo air brakes was equipped with shot-resistant Cordatic tires, the suspension provided by two-two semi-elliptic leaf springs at front and rear. The relatively wide track width (1700 mm) and the 3000 mm wheelbase also resulted in stable road holding in the field.

Modifications
A serious problem was that during the marches, the R/4 radio installed on the armoured cars provided only 20 kilometres range on flat and just 5 kilometres on mountainous terrain between the armoured cars and the higher command echelons.

■ 40 M. CSABA ARMOURED COMMAND/SIGNAL CAR

The Army ordered special designed command/signal vehicles, the 40 M. Csaba, for the reconnaissance units, which had a greater radio capacity. The main requirement for this model was to be very similar to the combat vehicle, to keep production simple and to avoid drawing special enemy attention to it. The HTI together with the Factory performed the task based on the standard 39 M. Csaba armoured car. The command vehicle received a smaller one-man turret with only one 8mm 34/37 M. Gebauer machine gun. To place the radios, the anti-tank rifle, its mountings and accessories fixed to the turret wall were removed from the turret. The fourth member of the crew became the radio operator instead of the gunner. For him, a seat was built between the driver's compartment and the turret. The commander was able to connect to all military radios at 100 km in RH telegraph mode and 160 km on medium wave. This was ensured by a frame antenna attached to four pneumatic support legs which could be lifted and retract. Only a dozen was built officially, though it is likely that a few damaged 39 M. were converted to command vehicles during the war.

▲ 39 M. Csaba armoured cars of the 2nd Reconnaissance Battalion during the operation in Transylvania, September 1940. The battalion had the circle size military insignia and the white F.2. unit sign stands for the 2nd Reconnaissance Battalion, the horizontal white bar represents the 1st Platoon of the Armoured Car Company. (Deák Tamás)

▼ 39 M. Csaba armoured car belonged to the 2nd Reconnaissance Battalion, battalion staff advancing in Transylvania September 1940. The white 2.F. was the unit sign, the T. stands for staff. Behind the armoured car is an ex-Polish Polski-Fiat 508 staff car. (War Correspondent Company)

▲ The 40 M. Csaba command/signal armoured cars employed as company and battalion command/signal armoured cars at the reconnaissance battalions. Factory fresh 40 M. armoured cars perform a test drive. (Fortepan/Korbuly)
Small photo: 39 M. Csaba armoured car belonged to the 1st Armoured Cavalry Battalion in the summer of 1941, passing a bridge in the Carpathian Mountains. (Deák Tamás)

39 M. CSABA ARMOURED CAR - HUNGARY 1941

▲ 39 M. Csaba armoured car belonged to the 2nd Reconnaissance Battalion wearing the circular military insignia, only used by the 2nd Reconnaissance Battalion during the campaign.

▲ The 39 M. Csaba armoured cars of the 2nd Reconnaissance Battalion had three-tone camouflage and circle size military insignia in September 1940. (Deák Tamás)

▶ The Ludovika Military Academy also got 39 M. Csaba armoured cars, during the summer exercises the armoured cars got a white L45 tactical number painted on the turret. (Mujzer collection)

▼ Advancing 39 M. Csaba armoured car of the 1st Reconnaissance Battalion at the Carpathian Mountains with octagonal military insignia. (Deák Tamás)

CAMOUFLAGE AND DISTINCTIVE SIGNS

The Hungarian armoured vehicles manufactured from 1940 were finished in French-style camouflage consisting of a base colour of dark olive green with light ochre and red-brown blotches. Until 1942, this disruptive camouflage was brush-applied with hard-edged patterns of irregular blotches. However, in 1942 the Hungarians began to use spray equipment, giving the camouflage patterns a more diaphanous appearance.

During the deployment of the 1st Armoured Field Division in 1942, the Hungarian made armoured vehicles; Toldi light tanks, Nimród self-propelled autocannons and Csaba armoured cars were repainted to "panzer" grey, similar to the Pz.IVF-1 and Skoda 38(t) tanks.

In 1944, some of the armoured and non-armoured vehicles were uniformly painted dark green. In April 1944, at least one Csaba armoured car platoon of the 2nd Reconnaissance Battalion was overpainted in German-style light ochre. In 1944, two to five 39 M. Csaba armoured cars were handed over to the mobile reserve of the State Police. The known two Csaba, RR-711 and -712 were painted dark bright blue.

NATIONAL MILITARY INSIGNIA

In 1940, temporary military insignias were developed by the battalions and the higher echelons. The 1st Reconnaissance Battalion used a white Maltese cross as a base in 1940. The green or red outlines and the circle were to be painted in different combinations for each company of the battalion. The insignia was painted on all four sides and, for aerial identification, onto the engine deck too. The Csaba armoured cars had the insignia painted onto the turret sides too. The vehicles of the 2nd Reconnaissance Battalion had a green cross outlined in white over a red circular base painted on five places, was allowed to use it up to the end of 1941.

Finally, Mobile Corps Command and the Institute of Military Technology jointly developed the octagonal insignia consisting of a green cross outlined in white and the area between the arms of the cross filled with red in 1941. It became the standard military insignia from 1941 until 1942. The insignia should be painted onto the sides, front, rear and the top (engine deck) of vehicles. The insignia in practice resulted to be too large and colourful. The insignia on the front hull, behind where sat the driver on Csaba armoured cars made a perfect aiming-point for enemy anti-tank gunners. Therefore, in the field crews often covered the front insignia with mud.

In November 1942 a new, insignia came into service, already used by the air force - white cross over a black square - authorised in three different sizes according to the location on the vehicles. The instructions required the insignia to be placed on all visible sides of vehicles, but in practice, it was applied only to the sides and in increased size to the engine deck.

UNITS INSIGNIAS

From 1938, each unit invented its own colourful unit identification signs. Later, the standard requirements were to use adaptations of easy geometrical symbols. As of 1942 the units started to use the basic geometrical symbols, painted on the front and back mud-guards or the hull. The Armoured Corps regulated the unit signs of the subordinated units in 1943. In 1944, the division and regiment (battalion) signs were painted on the left and right front and rear hull or mud-guards. The non-armoured vehicles also carried unit signs, following the above-mentioned regulations.

LICENSE PLATES

The armoured vehicles had painted licence plates. On the armoured cars, the front serial number was shown in a thin white rectangle. The style was usually a Pc. (abbreviation of the armoured car) with the national shield (red-white-green), followed by a three-digit serial number. The letters and the numbers were painted in black. The same serial numbers were on the rear of the hull but in a square shape. Later, from 1944, the front license plate was simply painted on the camouflage without white background.

■ TACTICAL NUMBERING

Hungarian armoured vehicles adopted the use of three-four digits turret numbers in 1942. The 2nd Reconnaissance Battalion used three-digit tactical numbers on the Csaba armoured cars, painted on the rear plate of the turret. The Ludovica Military Academy used big L and two digits tactical numbers on summer exercises.

■ SAMPLE OF UNIT INSIGNIA

 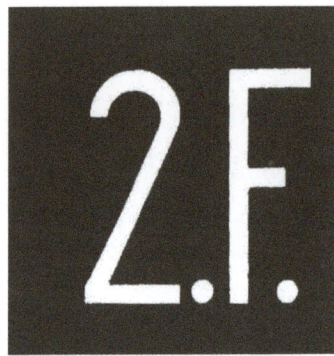 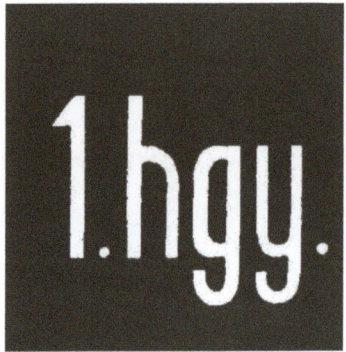

▲ 1st Reconnaissance Battalion 1940-1941 - 2nd Reconnaissance Battalion 1940-1941 - 1st Mountain Brigade, Armoured Car Platoon

▲ 2nd Reconnaissance Battalion 1942-1945 - 3rd Reconnaissance Battalion - Maltese cross insignia 1940

▲ Circular insignia 1940-1941 - Octagonal insignia 1941-1942 - White cross-black square insignia 1943-1945

40 M. CSABA COMMAND A.C. - GALICIA 1944

▲ 40 M. Csaba command/signal armoured car belonged to the 2nd Reconnaissance Battalion fought at Galicia in April 1944.

39 M. CSABA ARMOURED CAR - GALICIA 1944

▲ 39 M. Csaba armoured car belonged to the armoured car company of the 2nd Reconnaissance Battalion wears the dark yellow camouflage, during the operation around Nadworna, April of 1944, Galicia.

VERSIONS OF THE VEHICLE

- **Main variants: 39 M. Csaba armoured car**

Weight: 5,95 tonnes
Crew: 4 members (commander, gunner, driver, radio man, co-driver)
Armour: Front 13-mm, Side 9-mm, Rear 9-mm
Main armament: 1x20mm 36 M. anti-tank rifle
Secondary armament: 1x8 mm 34/37 AM. machine-gun
Engine: Ford G61T, 3560 cubic centimetre, 8 cylinders, water-cooled 90-95Hp petrol engine
Maximum speed on the road: 65 km/h
Autonomy: 150-200 km

- **Main variants: 40 M. Csaba armoured command/signal car**

Weight: 5,85 tonnes
Crew: 4 members (commander, radio operator, driver, co-driver)
Armour: Front 13-mm, Side 9-mm, Rear 9-mm
Main armament: 1x8 mm machine gun
Engine: Ford G61T, 3560 cubic centimetre, 8 cylinders, water-cooled 90-95Hp petrol engine
Maximum speed on the road: 70 km/h
Autonomy: 150-200 km

▲ Advancing command group of the 2nd Reconnaissance Battalion in Galicia with 40 M. Csaba command/signal armoured car Pc.408, surrounded by dispatch riders on Puch G350 motorbikes following Skoda and Mercedes staff cars. The Hungarians wearing whitewashed 35M steel helmets. (ECPA)

Further developments

During the war, the Hungarian Army intended to replace the Csaba armoured car with a better armed and armoured vehicle with better off-road capacity and low profile. It would be the Hunor armoured car, which unfortunately never left the design table, not even a prototype was built. The hull was similar to the German Fu. Kfz.67/Kfz.232 armoured car, which was designed in 1935. The chassis was asymmetrical three-axle, six-wheel type, with 11.00 x 20 shoot resistant Lypsoid tire. This tire with a raw rubber inner tube was one of Straussler's patents, but during the war, the purchase of natural rubber was already hopeless. The drive was powered by two V-8 petrol engines with 165 hp. The armoured car had front and rear driving compartments. The turret of the armoured car is situated in the centre of the chassis, armed with one-one 20mm canon and 8mm machinegun, which was not too powerful at that time. It had a crew of 3-4. The armoured car had two propellers at the rear of the chassis, could switch to amphibious mode, the flotation was provided by a rubberized hose attached to the side of the armoured car inflated by compressed air.

DATA SHEET		
	39 M. Csaba armoured car	40 M. Csaba armoured command/signal car
Length	4520 mm	4520 mm
Width	2100 mm	2100 mm
Height	2370 mm	2300 mm
Minimum hull height above ground		
Weight in combat order	5,95 tonnes	5,85 tonnes
Crew	4	4
Engine	Ford G61T, 8 cylinders, water-cooled 90-95Hp petrol engine	
Maximum speed		
Autonomy	150-200 km	150-200 km
Tank capacity		
Armour thickness	13-9 mm	13-9 mm
Armament	1x20mm anti-tank rifle, 1x8mm machine gun	1x8mm machine gun

▲ The 39 M. Csaba turrets were produced for the Hungarian River Forces, built on armoured minesweeper boats, called PAM in 1943. (Karai Sandor)

PRODUCTION

The Csaba armoured cars were exclusively produced by Weiss Manfred Factory at Csepel, a suburb of the Hungarian capital. According to the reports the Weiss Manfred Factory built 97 39 M. Csaba armoured cars and 20 40 M. Csaba command/signal armoured cars plus probably two more, altogether 119 armoured cars. After the war, 20 unfinished Csaba armoured car bodies were found in the yard of the Weiss Manfred Factory in the summer of 1945.

According to the distributed number plates the next armoured cars were produced and handed over to the armoured car companies:

-Number plates Pc.101-108 – 8 iron/training vehicles
- Pc.109-161 - 53 39 M. Csaba armoured cars
- Pc.163-181 - 19 39 M. Csaba armoured cars
- Pc.182-192 - 11 39 M. Csaba armoured cars
- Pc.193-198 - 6 39 M. Csaba armoured cars
- Pc.162 and Pc.182 converted 40 M. Csaba command/signal armoured car
- Pc.400-411 12 40 M. Csaba command/signal armoured car
- Pc.412-417, 6 40 M. Csaba command/signal armoured cars

Organisation

By mid-1940, the armoured units were re-organised following the delivery of the new 38 M. Toldi light tanks and 39 M. Csaba armoured cars to the troops in significant quantity. Within the Mobile Corps each motorised and cavalry brigade had one-one reconnaissance or armoured cavalry battalion. These battalions had a similar structure one-one armoured car, tankette and light tank companies. The reconnaissance battalions had one more motorised rifle companies, plus combat support and support detachments. Before the Barbarossa campaign, another re-organisation taken place.

The reconnaissance battalions had a one-one armoured car, motorcycle, motorised rifle and anti-tank companies plus one-one signal, sapper and maintenance platoons subordinated to the battalion staff. The armoured car company had 16 x 39 M. and 40 M. armoured cars, organised into three platoons, each had 5 armoured cars and one 40 M. Csaba command/signal armoured car belonged to the company staff. The anti-tank gun company had 4 x 37mm 36 M. (Pak36) anti-tank guns. The motorised rifle company had 12 x 8mm 31 M. Solothurn light machine guns, 3 x 20mm 36 M. Solothurn anti-tank rifles and 3X 8mm 07/31 M. machine guns. The motorcycle company was armed with 12 x 8mm 31 M. Solothurn light machine guns and 3 x 20mm 36 M. Solothurn anti-tank rifles.

The armoured cavalry battalions also had one armoured car company with 16 x 39 M. Csaba armoured cars, two tankette companies with 35 M. FIAT Ansaldo tankettes, one anti-tank gun company with 37mm 36 M. anti-tank guns and one-one signal, sapper and maintenance platoons subordinated to the battalion staff. The armoured cavalry battalions were also reinforced with 10 x 38 M. Toldi light tanks.

The 1st Hungarian Mountain Brigade also had one armoured car platoon in 1941. The armoured car platoon had 22 men 3 x 39 M. Csaba an armoured car, two motorcycles and one-one staff car and truck. The armoured car platoon was disbanded by the end of 1941.

From 1943, two different type reconnaissance battalion was organised, one for the new infantry divisions and one for the armoured and cavalry divisions. Following the new overall organisation, the Hungarian Army had eight first-line infantry divisions (each with three infantry regiments) and each of them had one-one assault gun and reconnaissance battalions too. The reconnaissance battalions belonging to the eight first-line infantry divisions consisted of one hussar and one bicycle company, and one platoon each of armoured cars (4 x 39 M. Csaba armoured cars), anti-tank gun (4 x 40mm 40 M. or 75mm 43 M./Pak40 anti-tank guns), mortar (4 x 81mm 36 M. mortars), signal and sapper. The armoured car platoons were rarely equipped with armoured cars due to the shortage of the 39 M. Csaba armoured cars.

The two armoured divisions also had one reconnaissance battalions each. The 1st Reconnaissance Battalion was stationed at Budapest, the 2nd Reconnaissance Battalion based at Kassa (Kosice) wearing the tactical numbers of their armoured divisions. These reconnaissance battalions were equipped with an armoured car company, a motorised rifle company (12 x 8mm 31 M. Solothurn light machine guns, 2 x 50mm 39 M. mortars, 2 x 20mm 36 M. Solothurn anti-tank rifles), a motorcycle company (12 x 8mm 31 M. Solothurn light machine guns, 2 x 20mm 36 M. Solothurn anti-tank rifles), anti-tank gun company (4 x 40mm 40 M. or 75mm 43 M./Pak 40 anti-tank guns), the battalion staff had one-one signal, sapper, maintenance platoons. The armoured car company had three platoons each had 4 x 39 M. Csaba armoured cars, one-one 40 M. Csaba armoured command/signal car served at the company staff and the battalion HQ. The 1st Cavalry Division included the 3rd Reconnaissance Battalion; its peacetime garrison was at Szilágysomlyó. The battalion had two armoured car companies with 26 x 39 M. Csaba armoured cars, and one anti-tank company (4 x 40mm 40 M. or 75mm 43 M./Pak 40 anti-tank guns), the battalion staff had one-one signal, sapper and maintenance platoons. The armoured car companies had three platoons each had 4 x 39 M. Csaba armoured cars, one-one 40 M. Csaba armoured command/signal car served at the company staff and the battalion HQ.

In 1944, the State Police and the gendarme also got some 39 M. Csaba armoured cars, the police vehicles were painted dark blue.

Operations

The armoured car units took part in all major Hungarian military operations during the war, the armoured car companies were exclusively equipped with the Hungarian designed and produced 39 M. and 40 M. Csaba armoured cars.

In 1940, Transylvania the armoured cavalry and reconnaissance battalions had received their 39 M. Csaba armoured cars fresh from the Factory, some of them at the assembly areas only at the last minute. The factory-fresh vehicles were incomplete and had a lot of mechanical failures.

The short Yugoslavian campaign was the baptism of fire of the Csaba armoured cars, the vehicles were deployed in the classic armoured car roles for reconnaissance, liaison, escort duties. The 2nd Cavalry Brigade sent 39 M. Csaba armoured cars under 1st Lieutenant László Béldy on 13 April, to explore the stronghold at Szenttamás (Srbobran). He was the company commander of the Armoured Car Company of 2nd Armoured Cavalry Battalion; he led his company towards Szenttamás when he noticed that the combat formation of his armoured car company became clumsy. He stopped the Company and ordered the troops to keep the proper formation. After this short stop, the Armoured Car Company continued with 1st Lieutenant Béldi's Csaba armoured car leading the company. A well-camouflaged 37mm Serbian anti-tank gun opened up on the advancing 39 M. Csaba armoured cars, the Pc.109 was hit five times, the Pc.118 was shot three times. 1st Lieutenant Béldi and his five men were killed, just two survived. Posthumously he was decorated with the Hungarian Knight Cross with swords.

During the Barbarossa campaign, the Csaba armoured cars served with distinction. One of the greatest achievements of the Csaba armoured cars connected to the battle around Uman in late July early August 1941, where the Hungarian Mobile Corps played a vital role to prevent the escape of the Soviet troops out of the encirclement. The 1st Cavalry Brigade took part in the successful operations against the Uman pocket. On 6 August, the commander of the brigade, Major General Antal Vattay, ordered the armoured cavalry battalion to reconnoitre the area around Golovanevsk, where the encircled Red Army units were located. The reconnaissance force consisted of one bicycle platoon and an armoured car platoon with three 39 M. Csaba armoured cars and was led by Ensign László Merész. The Ensign led two Csabas on the road to Moldovka, keeping the third in reserve with the bicycle platoon. The two advancing 39 M. Csaba armoured cars surprised two Cossack cavalry squadrons on the road, the 39 M. Csaba armoured cars opened fire from point-blank range and annihilated the soviet cavalry troops. Later on, Soviet motorised troops of 20 trucks and around 200 riflemen approached the killing fields on the road, trying to break through the encirclement. The Csabas opened fire again with their anti-tank rifles and machine guns. During the contact, the armoured cars exhausting their ammunition, firing 12,000 machine-gun bullets and 720 20mm shells. The Hungarian armoured cars succeeded in halting the Soviet troops of the 6th Army and sealed the gap in the encirclement. For his actions during this operation, Ensign Merész was decorated with the Great Gold Officer Bravery Medal.

▲ 38M. Toldi light tanks and 39 M. Csaba armoured cars of the 1st Reconnaissance Battalion with three-tone camouflage and white lightning bolt unit sign during a summer exercise in 1941. (Deák Tamás)

▼ Armoured car company of the 2nd Armoured Cavalry Battalion during the operation in Yugoslavia, April 1941. The 39 M. Csaba armoured cars were led by a Mercedes G5 command car. (Deák Tamás)

The 1st Reconnaissance Battalion was led by Lieutenant Colonel István Vaska, his unit belonged to the 1st Armoured Field Division. The 1st Reconnaissance Battalion took part in the summer bridgehead battles at the River Don in 1942. By that time the terrain and the determined enemy resistance did not favour the deployment of the armoured cars. Their weapons were too light and their armour protection too weak even against the Soviet anti-tank rifles. The technical losses of the 1st Armoured Field Division were ten 39 M. Csaba armoured cars during the campaign 1942-1943.

The 2nd Armoured Division was totally equipped with Hungarian produced armoured vehicles, among them were 14 x 39 M. and 40 M. Csaba armoured cars belonged to the 2nd Reconnaissance Battalion. On 13 April, the 2nd Reconnaissance battalion occupied the Lukwa passage and Rosulna and clashed with the Soviet rear guards west of Nadworna. The Hungarians lost one killed and three wounded and two 39 M. Csaba armoured cars, one 38 M. Botond truck and one car were destroyed.

The 3rd Reconnaissance Battalion belonged to the 1st Cavalry Division according some sources the battalion was deployed with only one armoured car company equipped with 13 Csaba armoured cars. After the re-deployment of the Cavalry Division, the 3rd Reconnaissance Battalion had only six armoured cars out of its original 23.

The 1st Reconnaissance Battalion fought with the 1st Armoured Division on Hungarian territory during 1944-1945. That time the battalion had one-one armoured, motorcycle and motorised rifle companies. The battalion was lack of the armoured car company and fire and combat support platoons. It had a composite armoured company where the 39 M. Csaba armoured cars and 38 M. Toldi light tanks of the Division were assembled.

During the siege of Budapest in 1944-1945, the Hungarian Police and the Gendarme units also had armoured subunits with antiquated 35 M. FIAT-Ansaldo tankettes and 39 M. Csaba armoured cars encircled in Budapest. The Galánta Gendarmerie Battalion had a few 39 M. Csaba armoured cars. The police forces were also involved in the defence of the city. The Police Assault Battalion launched a counter-attack against advancing Russian troops at Vecsés, Andrássy-telep on 1 November 1944. The police were supported by five 39 M. Csaba armoured cars. Soviets easily knocked out three 39 M. Csaba armoured cars during the battle.

The remaining 39 M. and 40 M. Csaba armoured cars were lost during the fighting in Hungary between 1944 and 1945. The left-behind knocked out or abandoned vehicles were collected as scrap metal for recycling. No information is available about existing Csaba armoured car, although one was presented at Moskva on the war trophy exhibition right after the war.

▲ 39 M. Csaba armoured car belonged to the 1st Armoured Cavalry Battalion wading a creek at the Carpathian Mountains. (Deák Tamás)

39 M. CSABA ARMOURED CAR - HUNGARY 1944

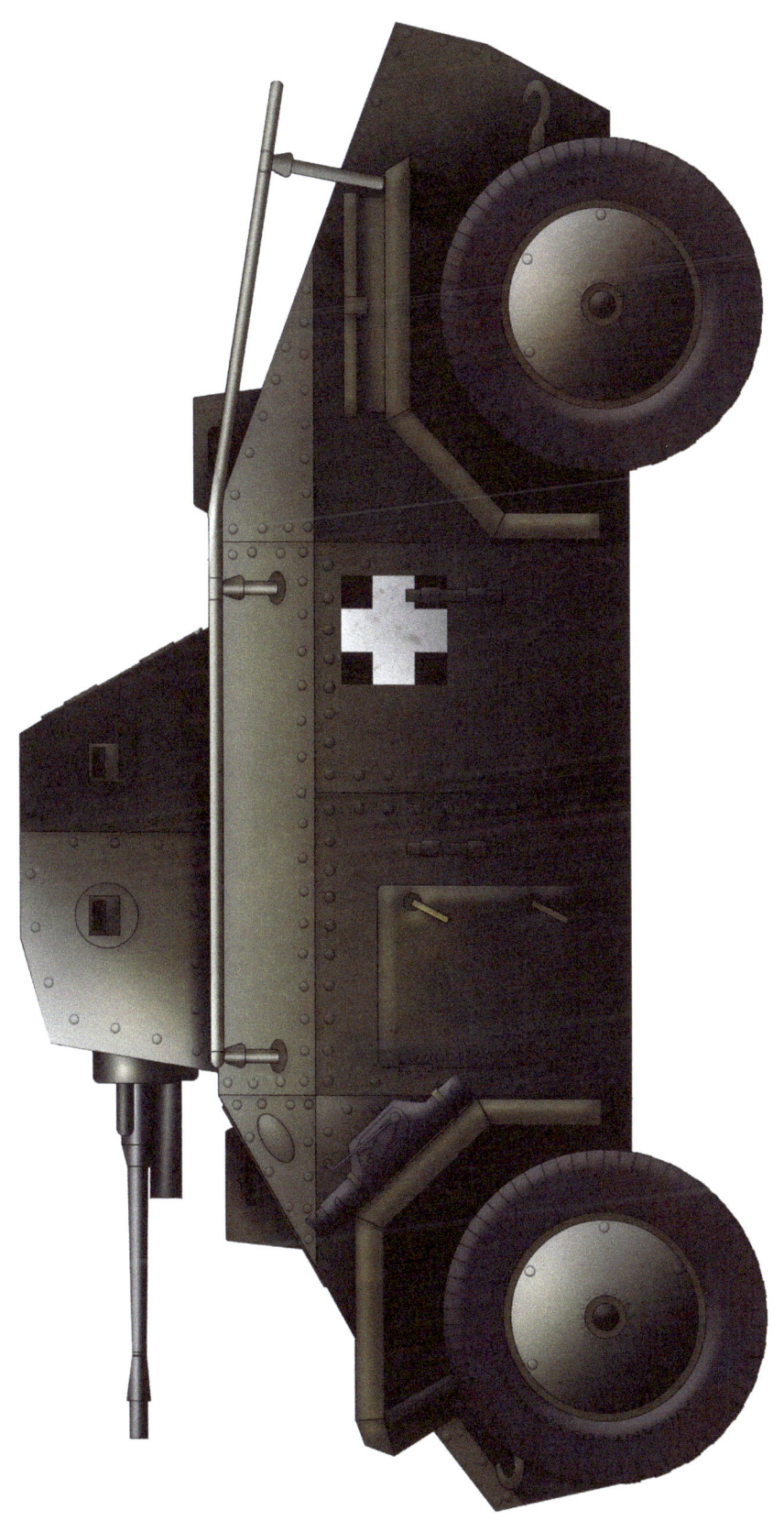

▲ 39 M. Csaba armoured car have the standard olive green camouflage with late style military insignia, probably belonged to the armoured car company of one of the reconnaissance battalion.

▲ 39 M. Csaba armoured car with dark olive-green camouflage and white cross–black square military insignia, parking at the yard of the Automobile Depot in 1943. (Deák Tamás)

▼ 39 M. Csaba armoured car in static observation position with light machine gun team armed with an 8mm 31 M. light machine gun and 35 M. rifles. (War Correspondent Company)

▲ 39 M. Csaba armoured car front and back view profile

▲ 39 M. Csaba armoured car front and back view profile

▲ Sand-yellow camouflaged 39 M. Csaba armoured car belonged to the 2nd Reconnaissance Battalion, April 1944 Nadworna, Galicia. (Deák Tamás)   ▼ Burned out 39 M. Csaba armoured car, P.125 belonged to the 1st Reconnaissance Battalion, shot out at Rogozna in July 1941. (Szollár János).

Great photo: On 17 April 1944 the troopers of the 2nd Reconnaissance Battalion watching the artillery preparation before the attack at Nadworna, Galicia. The armoured cars had three-digit tactical numbers started with 13, probably belonged to the 3rd Armoured Car Platoon/ Armoured Car Company. The armoured cars were painted in three-tone camouflage. (ECPA)

BIBLIOGRAPHY

- Dr Tamás Baczoni – Dr László Tóth: Hungarian Army Uniforms 1939 – 1945, HUNIFORM 2010
- Csaba Becze: Magyar steel, Mashroom Publication, 2006
- Dénes Bernád, Charles K. Kliment: Magyar Warriors, The history of the Royal Hungarian Armed Forces 1919-1945, volume 1-2, Helion Publication, 2015, 2017
- Bíró Ádám – Éder Miklós – Sárhidai Gyula: A magyar királyi honvédség hazai gyártású páncélos harcjárművei 1920- 1945, Petit Real, 2012
- Bíró Ádám: A 40/43M Zrínyi rohamtarack kifejlesztése és használata, 1-3. rész, Haditechnika 1996/1, 2 and 4
- Bíró Ádám: The AC-II, 39 M. Csaba páncélgépkocsik, Haditechnika 1992/3
- Bonhardt Attila: Zrínyi II rohamtarack, Pekó Kiadó 2015
- Bonhardt Attila – Sárhidai Gyula – Winkler Róbert: A magyar királyi honvédség fegyverzete 1919-45 part 1, Zrínyi, 1992
- Patrick Cloutier: Three Kings: Axis Royal Armies on the Russian Front 1941, 2014
- Éder Miklós: Magyar páncélos járművek alakulat jelzései, 1.-2. rész, Militaria Modell 1991 / 1-2
- Éder Miklós: 39 M. Csaba páncélgépkocsi, Militaria Modell 1992/1
- Éder Miklós: Magyar páncélosok hadi jelzése, 1917-1945, Militaria Modell 1992/6
- Hajdú Ferenc – Sárhidai Gyula: A magyar királyi honvéd Haditechnikai Intézettől a HM Technológiai Hivatalig, HM Technológiai Hivatal 2005
- Kovácsházi Miklós: A Zrínyi jármű család történte 1-2, Haditechnika 2013/6, 2014/1
- Charles Kliment- Vladimir Francev: Czechoslovakian AFVs 1918-1948, Schiffer, 1997
- Eduardo Gil Martinez: Fuerzas Acorazadas Húngaras 1939-43, Almena 2017
- Péter Mujzer: Huns on Wheels, Hungarian Mobile Forces in WWII, Armoured, Cavalry, Bicycle Troops, Motorised Rifle, Mujzer and Partners Ltd., 2015
- Péter Mujzer: Hungarian Armoured Forces in WWII, KAGERO Books, PHOTOSNIPER 26., 2017
- Péter Mujzer: Operational History of the Hungarian Armoured Troops in WW2, KAGERO, Photosniper 28., Lublin 2018.
- Péter Mujzer: Hungarian Soldier versus Soviet Soldier, Eastern Front 1941, Osprey Publishing, Oxford 2021.
- Péter Mujzer: Hungarian Arms and Armours of World War Two, KEY Publishing, Stamford 2021.
- Péter Mujzer: Barbarossa Campaign in 1941 Hungarian perspective, KAGERO, Lublin 2021.
- Leo Niehorster: The Royal Hungarian Army 1920-45, Bayside Books, 1998
- Nigel Thomas- László Pál Szabó: The Royal Hungarian Army in World War II, Ospery, 2008
- András Palásthy: Bapteme du feu mortel en Ukraine, Batailles&Blindes n.42
- Anthony Tucker-Jones: Armoured warfare and Hitler's allies 1941-1945, Pen&Sword, 2013

ALREADY PUBLISHED TITLES

ALL BOOKS IN THE SERIES ARE PRINTED IN ITALIAN AND ENGLISH

VISIT OUR WEBSITE FOR MORE INFORMATION ON
THE WEAPONS ENCYCLOPAEDIA:
https://soldiershop.com/collane/libri/the-weapons-encyclopaedia/

TWE-022 EN

www.ingramcontent.com/pod-product-compliance
Lightning Source LLC
LaVergne TN
LVHW072121060526
838201LV00068B/4940